PAJAMA PARTY

PAJAMA PARTY

AMY HEST

ILLUSTRATIONS BY
IRENE TRIVAS

MORROW JUNIOR BOOKS / NEW YORK

*For my Kate and for Ryan,
who are very fond
of pajama parties*
—A.H.

Pen and ink with watercolor and gouache paints were
used for the full-color artwork. The text type is
15½ point Tiffany Light.

Inquiries should be addressed to
William Morrow and Company, Inc.,
1350 Avenue of the Americas,
New York, N.Y. 10019.

Printed in the United States of America.

1 2 3 4 5 6 7 8 9 10

Library of Congress Cataloging-in-Publication Data

Hest, Amy.
Pajama party / by Amy Hest; illustrations by Irene Trivas.
p.   cm.
Summary: Casey, Jenny, and Kate have a pajama party complete with
sleeping bags, chocolate chip cookies, and scary stories.
ISBN 0-688-07866-4. —ISBN 0-688-07870-2 (library)
[1. Sleepovers—Fiction.   2. Friendship—Fiction.]   I. Trivas,
Irene, ill.   II. Title.
PZ7.H4375Paj   1992
[Fic]—dc20   91-13676   CIP   AC

Contents

Dear Reader...

This is the story of a pajama party. It is also the story of three good friends. One of them is me, Casey. One is Jenny Marks. And number three is Kate. In fact, Kate is my real best friend, but when I say it, Jenny gets mad. She shouldn't, though. A person can't have two best friends, or at least two best friends at the same time. Besides, Kate and I look nearly alike. Some people say we look like cousins, even.

1 *How We Break the News to Our Mothers*

It all started with my sister, Syd, who is thirteen. Now when Syd turned thirteen, it was some big deal. She went on like nobody in the *world* ever turned thirteen before. And she made herself a party: a pajama party for twelve of her closest friends.

Syd's party was something else. I know because she let me serve: popcorn, potato chips, warm-from-the-oven brownies. Not that I minded. Because,

between courses, I got to hang around that perfumed, hair-blowing room. That is, I got to hang around until somebody noticed, and it was usually Syd. "This is a *teenage* pajama party, so scram!" she'd yell.

"Teenage pajama parties are bad and

boring," I told Kate and Jenny the very next day. "All they do is eat junk food and play loud music and spray perfume and dance, dance, dance! Who'd want to go to a party like *that*?"

"Me," Jenny said. "When I'm thirteen, I will have one, too. You are both invited, and we'll stay up all night."

Kate thought about that. She thought a long time, and she hummed a little tune. Kate always hums a little tune when she is thinking something over. When she stopped humming, she started talking. "A person could have a pajama party anytime," she said. "Even when she's eight. She could invite two good friends, and they would call it a three-girl pajama party."

Good old Kate. She's always got the best ideas. Right away, we took a vote about where to have it, and we voted my house. We voted my house *after* I told them about the leftover brownies.

We found my mother in the kitchen, picking popcorn off the floor. "Next time Syd makes a party, there will be no popcorn," she said, tossing a piece into her mouth.

"Please can we have a three-girl pajama party," I cried, "here tonight?"

"Here?" she squeaked. "Will it be loud like Syd's?"

"No way." We shook our heads.

"Will you stay up all night?"

"Not us," we said.

"Will you dance so hard the neighbors call?"

"Never," we swore. "Cross our hearts!"

My mother scooped up popcorn and said, "You've got yourselves a deal."

We charged down the two flights to Kate's apartment.

Kate's mother was typing away in a corner in her bedroom. "We are planning a three-girl pajama party tonight at Casey's," Kate explained. "May I, Mama? May I go?"

Her mother laughed. "I wish *I'd* get
invited to a pajama party." She laughed
again. "Don't forget your toothbrush, Kate.
Although I know you'll never use it."

Kate licked her lips. "Are you sure I
can go?" she asked.

"Of course, my lamb! A three-girl
pajama party sounds grand and great!"

Jenny's mother was planting carrot seeds in a box on the terrace. Jenny's mother is always planting something on the terrace. "We are planning a three-girl pajama party, tonight at Casey's," Jenny called through the glass door.

Her mother stood up straight. She pulled off her planting gloves and pushed up her planting sunglasses and waved her plastic spoon in the air. She slid open the glass door. "You're awfully young," she said. "You'll eat too much, and you'll never get a proper night's sleep. I know all about pajama parties, I do."

"Please!" begged Jenny. "Please say yes!"

Her mother frowned—the kind of frown that makes your eyebrows go all crooked. But after a while she said, "Go ahead, try it. Although you are way too young."

Making the list was Kate's idea. "You need one," she said, "to make a perfect party." So we got to work at Jenny's kitchen table on *The First and Best Three-Girl Pajama Party: Rules to Remember.* When the list was finished, it looked like this:

1. Wear pajamas. No nightgowns allowed. (Jenny said it wasn't fair about the no-nightgowns rule. She was mad, I think, because Kate and I have matching rainbow flannels from Kid Boutique. So we made an exception, for Jenny's sake. But just this once.)

2. Bring something good to eat. Bring enough for everyone, and make sure it's a surprise. Put it in a large brown bag, and staple it closed. Mark the bag PERSONAL, DO NOT PEEK, AND THAT MEANS YOU, SO SCRAM!

(Kate reminded us the food ought to be junky.)

3. Bring a flashlight, one stuffed animal, and your favorite pillow. Bring a set of markers—no dried-up markers, either—a notebook with perforated pages, and a sleeping bag, if you have one.

(Jenny said she didn't, so we told her we could make one with extra sheets from the linen closet.)

Then we all took off, in order to get ready.

2 *Warming Up, Minor Snags, and How Three Good Friends Steer Clear of Trouble*

On the dot of seven, the doorbell rang. It was Jenny, and her mother, too. Jenny's arms were all filled up with her pink beach tote and a stapled brown bag marked PERSONAL, DO NOT PEEK, AND THAT MEANS YOU, SO SCRAM! Jenny's mother looked scared. She kept saying stuff like,

"Are you all right, dear?" and "Promise to call if you need me, honey." Jenny promised. Throwing kisses to her mother, she ran down the hall to my room.

When Kate came, she was singing a made-up song. Kate always sings made-up songs, and they are usually about a girl named Kate. This one was about a girl named Kate who was riding her pink pony to a three-girl pajama party. She wasn't sure she would stay the whole night, though. She would have to think it over.

We closed the bedroom door. Tight. Then we each went to a corner to change into pajama-party clothes. Kate and I wore the matching flannels, and that was pretty neat. But when I turned around and spotted Jenny in her nightgown, I couldn't help wishing I had one just like it. Her nightgown was lavender, and long to the

floor. "You look like a queen," whispered Kate. Jenny liked that, and from then on she went around calling herself Queen Jenny.

We couldn't wait to roll out our sleeping bags. First Jenny's had to be made up from old polka-dot sheets. Syd even agreed to help. When we were done, I had to admit it was a lot prettier than my sleeping bag, which is plain old olive-drab with two fat zippers that always get stuck.

But the real problem was this: Who would sleep in the middle? Kate thought she should, since the party was her idea. Jenny said she should, since polka-dot sheets weren't a real sleeping bag at all.

I said *I* should sleep in the middle, since the party was at my house, after all, and in my room. We took a vote, and I lucked out. I got the middle!

We had another problem, though. A cookie problem. You see, I had filled my brown bag with chocolate chip cookies— lots of them. This wouldn't have been trouble at all if Jenny hadn't brought the same thing. Then Kate opened her bag, and wouldn't you know, chocolate chips! She laughed and started tossing them like Frisbees. Then we said, "What the heck," and started eating. Cookies. Cookies. And more cookies. My mother had filled the red picnic thermos with ice-cold milk, and we

20

drank plenty. After a while I couldn't *look* at another chocolate chip cookie.

Neither could Jenny. She pushed and shoved the brown bags with her feet.

Kate? Well, she flopped down across her sleeping bag and across part of mine,

too. And she got all curled up the way you
do when you've got a stomach ache.

"Stomach ache?" I asked.

"I'm okay," she groaned, and I knew it
was a lie. But after a while she was—okay,
I mean.

3 *Three Good Friends Swing until Midnight*

We made marker pictures and taped them to the wall and voted Jenny's best. Jenny always makes the grandest pictures. Her people look like real people, not stick people with globs of marker hair, and her dogs look like real dogs, the kind you see around the city.

Sometime around eight, Syd announced, "Little-kid pajama parties are bad and boring. I'm gone!"

24

"Gone where?" we said.

"I'm spending the night at Tina's house."

The minute she left, Kate disappeared. To do a little surveillance, she said. In other words, snoop around my sister's room. She reappeared fast with a pile of Syd's hotshot records and her shiny guitar. We played the records, one at a time, back and front, and we danced around my room until the mirrors shook. My mother stopped

by twice to remind us about the neighbors.

Then Kate got a case of the giggles,
and she made up a song about chocolate
chip cookies. It went like this: "Give me,
give me, give me, give me CHOCOLATE
CHIP COOKIES!..." She strummed along

on Syd's guitar: *strum strum strum, strum strum strum.* But then the E string snapped. Kate's voice went scared and flat, and we stuffed the guitar back in Syd's closet and stuffed ourselves into our sleeping bags.

By this time we all had a case of the giggles. It was nine-thirty, maybe, or ten. My mother knocked on the door. Jenny's mother was on the phone, she said, to say Jenny could come home if she wanted.

"Home!" hooted Jenny. "Why would I go home if I can sleep on the floor in polka-dot sheets and eat chocolate chip cookies until my stomach hurts!" She hooted some more.

"Did *my* mother call?" asked Kate.

"She didn't," said my mother.

"Maybe I'll call her," whispered Kate, curling up with Bill, her bear.

"Are you sick?" I asked.

"Not exactly," she answered, "but maybe I'll call my mother."

"Later. Call her later," I said. "Right now we need a story, and *I'm* going to tell it." Then we turned off the lamp and made sure our flashlights were working, and I got started. The story was a little on the scary side, but Kate and Jenny are used to that. Scary stories are my specialty. Here's the story I told that night:

29

"There were these good friends who sneaked out of their apartment house in the middle of the night. They were headed for the all-night ice cream parlor, and it was way downtown. Way, way downtown. But halfway there, this big storm appeared, like from nowhere. The wind blew. The streets were deserted. Meaning one hundred percent deserted. The sky was blackest-black, and tall, fat trees made weird and crazy shadows up and down the block. Suddenly there was a loud smashing noise! Someone screamed! And…"

"Quit!" cried Jenny in the dark. And I did. Because, to tell you the truth, this story was getting a little too scary even for me. I turned on the light.

Kate was gone.

4 How We Go from a Three-Girl Pajama Party to a Two-Girl Pajama Party

We found her in the kitchen with my mother. Kate was crying. Jenny gave her a hug. "Come on back to the party!" she said.

But Kate was slumped across my mother's lap, and her eyes were blotchy-red. "I want to go home," she said. "I want to go home *now*."

"You can't," I said. "This is a three-girl pajama party. If you go home, the party's ruined!"

"I don't care," she said, and I knew she meant it.

My mother kept on patting Kate's long hair. I wasn't crazy about that, and I called Kate a baby, even though I knew I shouldn't. My mother gave me a look. "Kate is just a little homesick," she said, "that's all."

Well, *I* knew *that*, so I told Kate, "You can sleep in the middle sleeping bag."

"I want to sleep in my bed," she said, "in my room."

"I know!" Jenny cried. "We'll take another vote on our marker pictures, and we'll vote yours best!"

Kate sniffed.

"Then how about if you sing another song," I said, "and we won't say a word about who broke the string on Syd's guitar!"

"A broken string on your sister's guitar?" My mother made one of those sucking-in whistle sounds. She didn't holler, though.

Kate blew her nose.

"Is there *anything* you want?" asked
my mother.

Kate licked her lips. She stood up tall
and stamped her foot. "I want to go home,"
she said. "I want to go home *now*!"

Kate's mother came over in her robe.
She kept on hugging Kate. "I remember my
first pajama party," she said. "I ate so
much, my stomach hurt. My mother came
and got me in the middle of the night, and
we took two subways and a bus to get home."

I wouldn't say good-bye to Kate. I knew I should, but I was mad. Kate was a quitter, a flat-leaver, and she'd ruined everything. One thing was certain: I was never going to speak to *her* again!

Jenny and I dragged ourselves back to the bedroom, but nothing was the same. We pulled my sleeping bag and her polka-dot sheets extra close and crawled inside. My zipper got stuck halfway up.

"How about a story?" she said, sticking her flashlight in my eyes.

"I don't know any more stories," I told her. "Want to draw some pictures?"

"I'm tired." Jenny yawned. "But I'm not going to sleep. The most important thing about a pajama party is staying up all night."

I rolled onto my stomach and patted the empty space next to me and thought about the way Kate looked all crumpled over on my mother's lap. And I was a little sorry I'd called her a baby.

"You know," I said to Jenny, "a two-girl pajama party isn't as good as a three-girl pajama party, but we could try again. We could try again at Kate's house, maybe. What do you think?"

Jenny didn't answer. She was fast asleep.

...Until Next Time

So much for the pajama party! But guess who showed up early the next morning? *Kate*. She showed up so early, in fact, she had to shake our sleeping bags to wake us up. But we didn't mind. Especially me.

Kate had brought a bag of muffins from the bakery and little containers of milk with straws from the deli. "It's a party," she said, laughing like crazy.

I was going to say something about

being her real best friend, but I knew
Jenny would get mad.

So I ate my muffin instead.